How to Knock Out Nightmares

How to Knock Out Nightmares

Catherine Leblanc

Roland Garrigue

INSIGHT KIDS

San Rafael, California

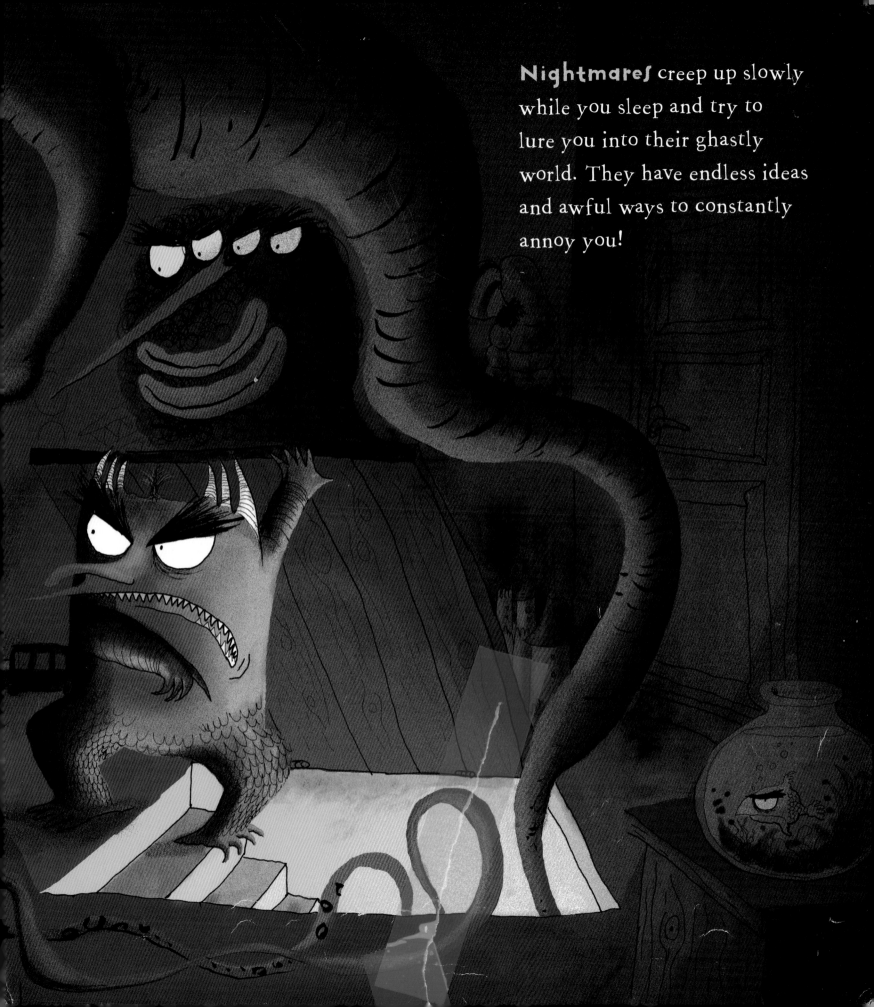

Nightmares creep up slowly while you sleep and try to lure you into their ghastly world. They have endless ideas and awful ways to constantly annoy you!

The terrible things nightmares do:

Even if you try to run away, a nightmare will hang on to you . . .

To suck you up a giant straw or launch you into outer space!

As soon as you try to build something,
the nightmare will destroy it!

A nightmare can have lots of fun trying to embarrass you . . .

. . . or chasing you around your bedroom
and threatening you in a million different ways!

A nightmare can separate
you from your friends,
family, and loved ones,
or force you into terrible places
filled with scary,
terrifying creatures!

Nightmares can change the way you look,
make toads crawl out of your mouth,
or take control of both your arms!

They can also set off the worst of disasters!
Earthquakes, floods, explosions . . . or even the end of the world!

How to defend yourself against nightmares:

Wake up! Waking up is the ultimate weapon.
Once you're awake, the danger is gone!
The nightmare loses all power and can no longer scare you.

In the morning, draw the nightmare as best you can.
Then scrunch up the paper and throw it in the trash.
This will turn your scary nightmare into a crybaby!

Think of a story that is nicer and much more fun!

At night, drink some herbal tea,
sprinkle confetti all around your bed,
and post a sign that says:
"No More Nightmares!"

NO
MORE
NIGHTMARES!

You can also create a secret spell and say it seven times.
You can lay out some nightmare traps,
such as placing a sugar cube on your nightstand
to attract some sweet dreams . . .

Also, you can make a dream catcher to put under your pillow.
This will stop nightmares from wanting to visit you.

As soon as a nightmare approaches,
the dream catcher will grab it by the ear,
and wipe the floor with it.

The smartest thing to do is to take that
nightmare and use it to your advantage!
Telling your friends about your
bad dreams makes for a great story time!

If some nightmares keep coming back despite all these protective measures, they must be trying to send you a message . . . Maybe they're pointing out something you don't like anymore, even if you're trying really hard.

For example, if you're too scared to tell your parents that you don't want to go to your violin lesson . . . the nightmare might make you practice all night!

If you understand the message
and choose to face your fear,
the nightmare will leave you
and allow room for pleasant dreams.

The End

To Clémence and Louane, for easy, restful nights.
—CL

INSIGHT
KIDS

PO Box 3088
San Rafael, CA 94912
www.insighteditions.com

Find us on Facebook: www.facebook.com/InsightEditions
Follow us on Twitter: @insighteditions

First published in the United States in 2014 by Insight Editions.
Originally published in France in 2013 by Éditions Glénat.
Comment Ratatiner les Cauchemars?
by C. Leblanc and R. Garrigue © 2013 Éditions Glénat
Translation © 2014 Insight Editions

Thanks to Christopher Goff and Marie Goff-Tuttle
for their help in translating this book.

Library of Congress Cataloging-in-Publication Data available.

ISBN: 978-1-60887-342-5

ROOTS of PEACE   REPLANTED PAPER

Insight Editions, in association with Roots of Peace, will plant two trees for each tree used in the
manufacturing of this book. Roots of Peace is an internationally renowned humanitarian organization
dedicated to eradicating land mines worldwide and converting war-torn lands into productive farms
and wildlife habitats. Roots of Peace will plant two million fruit and nut trees in Afghanistan and
provide farmers there with the skills and support necessary for sustainable land use.

Manufactured in China by Insight Editions

10 9 8 7 6 5 4 3 2 1